LOVE YOU TO THE MOON AND BACK

EZHILHARISH

ISBN 979-888521350-9

"Dedicated to my darling daugthers "Shankari VinothKumar" and "Dharshini VinothKumar""

Contents

Preface   *vii*

 1. Mails Of Introduction   1

 2. God's Plan   16

 3. "professor?"   23

 4. Chapter 4   28

 5. "bullets"   34

 6. Chapter 6   39

 7. Chapter 7   43

 8. Chapter 8   46

 9. Chapter 9   51

10. Chapter 10   55

11. "fear Not Baby Girl"   59

Preface

Some thoughts never leave us to sleep. It runs like a hungry lion and never stops until it is written in the paper. This story is very special as it was written with my younger one in my womb and elder one in my lap. Most of the chapters are typed with my elder on sleeping in my shoulder. The whole story started with the idea of falling in love with a person whom we never met before.

1
Mails of Introduction

♥1 Mailing A Stranger

Hlo Mugilan,

It's kind of weird that I am mailing someone whom I have never met in my life, but ended up to accept that we are getting married in next 6 months. Sorry, forgot to introduce myself, I am "Nila". Yes, I am the one who our parents tied you up within one hour of our birth. At first I thought they are playing pranks on me, but when they showed me the photos took on the day of our birth I couldn't take it that as a silly one.

I am not sure, how you are taking this. But I am seriously feeling weird. Don't take me wrong that I am saying this as weird, just think this whole thing from my shoes. A girl living a very normal life with her family and suddenly getting announced that she is getting married in six months with a Police Officer who is miles away, who she never met, who she never spoke with. See the irony, they said only way to contact you is this mail ID. I am not sure how you are taking all this marriage stuff, but I am kind of confused. I wish I get to know about you a little before getting into the marriage.

Regards,
Nila MSc., MPhil.,
Assistant Professor,
NIT Madras.

♥2 Being Honest

Dear Nila,

I am extremely sorry for starting this relationship in such a manner. I completely understand how you feel at present. I don't want to lie to you. I wish to be honest with you. I know about this from my 15[th]birthday. They reveled it to me in a fear that I may bring some other girl in to the picture. When they reveled, I got angry. But when they gave me the details, I felt it as interesting. All I got is your birthday photos, you cutting cake surrounded by your friends and family. Every year, it is my birthday gift from my parents from my 15[th]birthday. They revealed your name at my 18[th]birthday.

I started accepting you into my life, even though we haven't met each other. It may feel dumb, but I always have a big trust with my parents' choice. The school they chose for me, the college they chose for me, the career they chose for me, every single thing ended up as a best for me. I hope you are best for me.

I was always afraid of one thing, what if you reject your parents word and stop this arrangement. I asked my mother to give you my mail id, when she said we are supposed to get married in next 6 months. Though in a rush of excitement I asked her to give the mail id, I was horrified that you will mail me that you don't want to marry me. But from your words, I clearly got to know that you respect your parent's words, just as I do. I am happy that you want to know about me.

I am a police officer, working in a remote place. That's the reason, I was not able to give you any phone number or Telephone number. I can use the phone once in a month while reporting the head office, will try to call you when I get a chance. I am a Criminology graduate from The Bangalore university. I have a big set of friends, from my school days. They all know about you. Hope you will meet them before meeting me.

I am not sure how much you know about the reason why we are getting tied up. But I have been told that, both our Fathers are thick friends and so our mothers. To their surprise, we both were born on the same date and time in same hospital. That day, to keep the friendship long lasting they all decided to tie us both in marriage. Due to various reasons, my father was kept transferring from place to place. But wherever he goes, he always posted a letter from that address to your fathers. Due to your education and also your mother's illness, you father never got a chance to visit us. I remember your father visiting us when my grandmother expired few years ago. Please don't be angry on them, they hid this from us because, it may spoil our education and career. They love us more.

Even I wish to know more about you, I am personally happy that you are working in NIT. Take care.

Regards,

Mugilan♪

♥3 Sharing Things

Hlo Mugilan,

Received your mail yesterday, I was thinking the whole yesterday what I should reply you. After much thoughts, I decided to share some of my general details.

I am a Chemistry graduate and specialized in Forensic. Having my mother's health condition in mind, I chose to teach after working in field for 2 years. Still handling few cases when needed. I have 5 close friends. We 5 have nothing in common, other than we studied in same school. I am a chess player, also coaching three students in my free time. This is my professional details I think.

I am not an early morning person, I wake up on time and finish things with my schedule. I never like to wake up early. We have a little guy in our family, named June. He spends most of his time with my mom. In weekends, I am his partner to ride the streets of our city.

Thanks for the information about our parent's history. I was not aware of this much. All I was told is, you are my father's best friends son and Its been decided on the day I was born. I too haven't asked them much, as I was already struck with a bigger shock. I never had time in my life for new people, as I am always busy with already know ones. I spend one weekend of the month with my friends at some random spot which they choose. Two alternate weekends, I engage myself with my higher studies. I only get one-week end at home, it will move with family. I don't get much time to think out of all these. But when suddenly, I was introduced to this relationship, first thing I was afraid was how am I going to manage my timings. What if I spoil this one, which my parents are expecting to be successful? But after seeing your mail, I think you will help me to work this out.

I have idea about job nature, as I work with police men in my profession. I am interested to know more about your career and professional life. Not that I am not interested in your personal life. It's just that we can start with easy one.

Take care. Stay healthy!!
Regards,
Nila Msc., MPhil.,

Assistant Professor,
NIT Madras.

♥4 Pushing Questions

Dear Nila,

Happy to know about you. You are lucky that you have time to think about what to reply after reading my mail. But I don't get much time to think before replying. I get only one hour to visit this internet café, within that I have to finish my professional works and also pick words to reply your mail. This is nature of work here. We have some community clashes between two villages, me and my team mates are trying to bring down the violence between them. No guarantee that we get to finish this issue. I am not sharing this to scare you, but to reveal my actual condition here.

Regarding my profession, I am experienced in this field for past 5 years. First I was deployed in Delhi, I handled a riot case there. It gave a good start, seeing my performance and decisions one of my higher official suggested me to get moved to the place where I am working now just 3 months before. I am giving my best here.

Your life seems to be more vibrant and scheduled unlike mine. I am alerted and stay conscious 24/7. I just like being this way. Taking risk in saving lives and making things which change life of people, it always excites me. I love the job I do. I guess you have met my mom and dad. I also guess you would have understood, how much my mom hates my job. But she loves me much. Hope you will not take my mom's side on hating my job.

I love riffle shooting from my school days, have many medals for the same in all levels. I love collecting different type of rifles, especially the older ones. That's my favorite hobby. I think now we both know at least a little about each other. I also think, this question still can take time to be served here. Still I wish to ask you this, are you ready to marry this complete stranger? Just answer me when you wish to answer the same.

Take care.
Regards,
Mugilan♪

♥5 Adding To Prayer

Hlo Mugilan,

Was little afraid not getting your mail for about 5 days, now I get to know that you can access your mail once in a week i.e. on Saturday. I am never taking your mother's side on hating your job. Do what you love to do.

I wonder, how you are managing there for food and safe shelter. But I hope you are taking care of yourself in a good way. Though I am not afraid or worried about your work, I am adding you in my prayers. I always believe peoples prayer are stronger than anything in the world. Just don't think I am a big god person, I believe in an energy which is higher hand than all of us. Just be careful.

As you said about your riffles collection I wish to see them, hope you will show them after our marriage. Inspite of all my works, I have the habit of reading children's book. Specially Sudha moorthy, Enid Blyton books. They kind of stay as a stress buster in my life so far. I need at least 5 to six pages just before my sleep. They are the magic, you know. Mention if you have any favorite authors, will try.

I am not getting enough points to discuss, just ask me something which you want to know about me. Just tell me any incident or experience from your work. Just share me only If you have time to type all those.

At present I am in a hill station with my friends. We are planning some campfire and paragliding. My dear friends want to say a big HI to you and they all are whole heartedly welcoming you to join our gang.

Take care.

Regards,

Nila.

♥6 Post Script

Dear Nila,

Thanks for understanding my job. Just convey my greetings to your friends. Also convey that I am much happy to join your gang.

Don't worry about my food and safe shelter, I am having some villagers who helps me. They are supporting the police as they too wish to stop this clash. As you have asked any incident, I thought that "Why not share my current mission".

There are two different caste people here with a one common temple. Following the steps of the old people, one is feeling superior and don't want to allow the other caste people inside the temple. The younger ones of the suppressed caste people don't want to be the same lower ones just like their ancestors. In a rush of the emotions, they stole the goddesses' statue of the temple, which is still not found. The superior ones invaded the lower one's place and ruined everything. This made the issue worse, the young clan don't want to return the goddesses. The younger ones of the superior side, wants to make peace and they are helping us here. But the elder ones are not ready for the peace, this worsens the condition here. We as the police unable to handle the death count day by day. Handling daily missing cases and dead people makes us tiered unable to find the solution.

Like this we will be held for sometimes. But according to me, there is a solution for every problem. I believe that the solution is not long away, we hope to find it soon.

I just wanted to know what expectations you had for your future husband. Don't take me wrong in this, just want to make sure "How much disappointment I am going to bring in your life". Hey! My mom's birthday lies on 1ˢᵗJuly, convey my wishes to her. Stay happy and Take care

(P.S. – You haven't answered my question from last mail, "are you ready to marry this complete stranger?")

Regards,

Mugilan♪

♥7 Expectation

Dear Mugilan,

Guess where I was today? Took 2 days off, visited your home. Gave a birthday surprise to your mother. I don't know how you are feeling, leaving them alone here. But I could see that they are feeling alone and little disturbed. I just planned to visit them with my friend Shradha, after visiting them I found that just visiting them bought much happiness into their world. They miss you. Try to finish the issues soon and bounce back soon.

I am happy that you spoke about your current mission. I just thought of this, why don't you meet the younger ones of the suppressed people and explain the motive of the younger ones of the superior ones. May be this will help.

My expectations on my future husband, you may mock at me for my answer. I never thought I will get married. I am a first bench student with good contacts with professors and management, in both school and college. So everybody will maintain 10 steps gap between me. After coming to work, I was engaging myself with new tries and ideas. Never thought that I will marry and settle one day. So no idea about the husband thing. Thinking now about giving my hand to someone for the rest of life, I think there should be zero expectations. Because life partner is not the car we buy to work for us. I think you got what you wanted from me. Just posting the same question in your court. Just shoot your answer.

Take care.

(P.S. I answered your question in the very next mail dear Police Officer)

Regards,

Nila.

♥8 Decoding Answers

Dear Nila,

I am not sure, how much thank you should I send you. Not for just visiting them but also for talking on my behalf to my parents (My dad mailed me regarding your visit). He said you are taking my side, even before meeting me. He thinks I already made you fall for me, poor him. Thank you so much Nila ma, I am really happy that you cooked for her and listened to all her old stories, which me and dad usually feels bored about. Thank you so much...

About your same question, well before I started to think a girl in my life, they finger pointed you as the one for my life. All I had is the curiosity, how you will be looking, what you will be doing, etc. etc., so haven't got a chance to think about expectations and all. And I am happy that you are the one I am going to get tied up with.

About your suggestion, I am happy that you thought something for me. Will try to apply this. Arranging the meeting may be little dangerous, still why not take chance if that will work. Thank you for this too.

Week by week, I am getting to feel you closer to me. Your words are just ringing in my head but with my voice. Wish to hear your voice soon. Take care. And thanks again for visiting those elder ones.

(P.S. – Will definitely show you my riffle collections, sometimes even the police men become dumb. I am no exception for the same.)

Regards,

Mugilan♪

♥9 Our Family

Dear Mugilan,

We are working on a jewelry theft case, just held up with the case. Also took some time to process few things in my mind along with the case.

I am happy that you considered my idea, I prayed that the meeting should go on smoothly not affecting anyone. Don't forget to mention what happened in the next mail.

In our gang of 5, we have this rule "No Thank you and No Sorry". Actually we never sat and framed it, eventually we never said that. I feel that you don't need to thank me for what I did for our family. You are in our gang now; you are pledged to follow that one unwritten rule.

Regarding your expectations, I am feeling sorry for you. All your friends would have enjoyed with too many options, when you are struck with me. Just be honest, have you never felt frustrated about this child engagement. Feeling pity for you pa. I have one silly question for you, have you imagined any worst case about me? Like, I turned out to be a rude, self-pride, arrogant something worse. How would you have managed?

I am also happy that you are feeling closer to me within few weeks of the conversation, I think friendship of our parents blessed us for this. Even I wish to hear your voice soon. Also praying that the issue over there get smoothened soon.

(P.S.- I had no idea that uncle will mail you, but I am happy that he did. Small correction, why poor him? May be

he is right!!. Guessing my Police Man is not that dumb)
Regards,
Nila.

♥10 Love

Dear Nila,

Hope that the robbery case is resolved. Also take care of your health in mid of your schedules, I know how tough is to be on two professions at a time. Coming to your idea on the issue here, seriously you are that fairy with magic spells. Taking your words, I spoke with them and arranged a meeting regarding the same. The meeting went great. They both helped us to find the key persons who are involved in abducting the innocent people and the suppressed one are ready to give the statue back with the promise that they will be allowed inside the temple. Superior ones gave their promise that they will never ever treat them as their elders did. I guess within one or two month this condition will be back to normal peace and mainly equal than ever before. All credits to your idea.

Don't be sorry for me, actually I was relieved big from the issue every boy had in my age. Staying single and watching every girl crossing with the search that "Is she the one for me?" is the big task actually. But I was saved from that. I also will not lie that I haven't saw any girl, but every time I see a girl all I had in my thoughts were, how my Nila will be looking, long hair or shorter? Big doe eyes or small pretty ones? First rank holder or average one? Science one or arts one? Preferring Indian costumes or western ones? Like this, I will have many questions in my mind. I was not able to judge you with just a birthday pic. But I never wasted my time on many girls as I was born with a one for me. About your silly question, actually I was ready to accept whatever you are. I had a mindset that I can pamper any type of person. I also always believed my mother's words, "Nothing in this world left undefeated for the weapon named LOVE".

I will be visiting the headquarters this Tuesday, hope to have a call with you. Don't have any higher expectation, I am very bad in conversing directly and I will not be having much time to talk. Waiting to hear your voice. Take care.

(P.S. – Your Police man is not that dumb da Nila ma)

Regards,

Mugilan♪

♥11 Feels Good

Dear Mugilan,

Really happy that the issue is getting resolved and I guess within few weeks you will be moving to your normal routine. I take this as my prayers are answered. Waiting for the Tuesday, I don't think you are bad in conversations. I know you will not be able to read this mail before Saturday, still felt like mailing you. It feels good to send something in my mind to you.

Take care.

Regards,

Nila.

♥Conversation

M : Hello,

N : Yes,

M : Am I speaking to Nila?

N : Yes you are, May I know who is on the other end?

M : Nila ma,

N : Mugilan?

M : Yes, How are you?

N : Doing good, How are you? How is the village over there, hope all the problems are wrapped up for good.

M : Yes, All credits to you.

N : No, No, its because of those younger ones who decided to leave the bad traditions behind the valuable humanity.

M : May be, still your idea played as key, I should give that credit to you.

N : Mmmmm

M : So,

N : So?

M : Thought about any question, to throw in my court?

N : Actually yes, why do you use that music symbol in your email signature?

M : Thought that you will never ask me this question,

N : I got this doubt, from the first mail you sent me. I was always postponing it for a right time,

M : Mmmmm, That is not a big secret. I always love music, even learned the basics of Carnatic music. Do you love music?

N : Why not, but not like others always with the headset. I have my home theater setup and my favorite playlist which gets updated every month. Tell me your favorite composing will try to hear and add to my listing.

M : Sorry Nila ma, I have to go, will continue this conversation in mail. Bye Take care.

N : No issues carry on. Bye. Take care.

Dear Mugilan,

Though it was not a long call, I feel like I recognize your voice somewhat. But not sure, where I heard the same. Now I understand how hard it is for your parents to be far from you. I myself who haven't even met you in person so far, miss you sometime here. No wonder they miss you. I received call from one of your friends yesterday, they are planning to visit me on this Friday it seems. I am little nervous, maybe deep down my heart I want to make a good impression on first visit. The remaining week is really going to be hectic with work and new winds coming through my window.

Regards,
Nila

♥12 Missing Part

Dear Nila,

I should be honest with you Nila, my parents have got used to missing me. I will try my best not to place you in the shoes as them. But my profession is like that, not allowing me to settle in one place. I work in places where the safety is a big question mark, which always make me to leave the loved ones behind. I always take risky and challenging role. I always believe in my instincts and strength to handle my situations. It's not that I am selfish or over confidence. I just want to be a perfect man in my profession. Still I am concerned about my loved ones so I always keep my personal details hidden and it always force me to leave them behind in dark. I can never make that missing part disappear.

I know that they will reach you, I am the one who gave your number to them. Hope the meeting went well. I can understand how much hectic your schedules have become now days because of me. Take enough rest and Take care of yourselves.

(P.S – Hope that scar on your right hand elbow is fine now)

Regards,
Mugilan♪

♥13 Need Your Answers

Dear Mugilan,

Really a rough week, held up with a case involving the child trafficking. Only evidence we got was the soil sample, car prints and series of 4 children's corpse. Only yesterday we found all the hotspot and rescued nearly 14 children. Lost sleep for nearly 6 days. Slept at yesterday evening 6.00 and just woke up an hour ago.

I met your friends, they are so nice. Had nearly a conversation of half an hour. They shared your secrets, so from on be afraid of us or we will spill your beans. Just seeing your friends, I can say you are an open minded and happy go person.

I totally understand your condition over there in your profession. Missing someone is not happening for everyone. Having someone to miss us, means we have someone to love us. Don't feel bad for being a Perfect man in your profession. Be who you are, you will always have a one to love you for what you are.

(P.S – Need your answers when we meet in person how you know about a scar in my right hand elbow)

Regards,
Nila.

♥ Last Mail

Dear Wife,
Be ready to get all your answers soon.
Regards,
Mugilan♪

2
God's Plan

❦

Waiting for his next mail, her days moved little slow. She was not behaving normal like before. Her work was the only thing that moved her every day. The thought that he knows something more about her which she never revealed to anybody made her little nervous and more crazy. He simply mailed her "Be ready to get all your answers soon", but that really ate her mind and time.

Couple of Saturdays passed without his mail in her mailbox. As days passed she called his father few times, he assured that Mugilan will be safe. As days passed her curiosity changed into fear. Many what if's started to run in her mind. What if the issue got reborn and it costed his safety? What if he was assigned into something more dangerous resisting him from contacting her? She continued her prayers and daily life, keeping her thoughts around him.

Checking her to-do list of the day, she came out of her room to pick her tiffin box from dining table. She felt someone behind her and turning around she found just the wooden door. Scolding her wrong intuitions, she packed her things to work. Called her father to inform that she is leaving. Safely securing the house keys in her bag, she moved to her vehicle. Already June was waiting for her there. Usually she used to play with him for few minutes before starting from home. With a very bad mood, she just caressed his hair and started her vehicle. All the way to her college, she felt like someone is following her. In the parking lot, she confirmed that someone is behind her.

With a second of realizing, she took her gun and arrested the unknown figure's neck into her arms. Just a snap, she was ready to break his neck. "Nila, this is Mugilan." Hearing the statement, she tightened the grip. "Tell me on which day I mailed you first", her hold on him was like, If he answers wrong he is going to take a last word on the earth. "It's Thursday Nila ma, I promised to show you my rifle collection, never expected to see you with a one." Hearing the statement, she left the grip and kept the gun back safely. "Sorry Mugilan, I am very sorry for making the first meet horrible", that's the moment she saw him for the first time. He was adjusting his dress. She was rehearsing many things in her mind, how to talk or what to talk while meeting him for first time. Everything got messed up because of her stupid action.

Mugilan standing there folding his hand infront of her, unable to believe that He is finally meeting her in person. He purposely stopped mailing her so he can surprise her while meeting her. He thought of coming and introduce himself to her, but within that she held his neck pointing gun. He never expected to have a meet like this. Now holding much guilt in her eyes, punishing her lips for the mistakes she did, she was nervously playing with her ID card.

"Nila, Relax... It's my mistake I should have informed you beforehand, I thought to surprise you, but got myself surprised with your strong hold." She gave a staring look, making Mugilan to smile at her. "Sorry Mugilan, recent times are not playing nice on me, just was in conscious. Really sorry" she apologized sincerely. "Ok sorry accepted. I am staying here in a hotel. Just finish your works and give me a call, will come and pick you up. Take care", saying so he pulled her into his arms for a quick hug. A second of his warmth, reminded her something. But before she could react, he left her and started to move towards the exit of parking lot. Remembering that she doesn't have his phone number, she thought of calling him back. But a message tone from her phone diverted her. There smiled a message, "You can save this number as "My Police Man" dear wife - Mugilan♪". Not to disappoint her lovely police man, she saved his number and bounced back to her work.

During lunch, her father called her and informed that Mugilan is here in the town. She informed that she met him at morning and promised to get back home as soon as possible. Around 3 she wrapped up all her works, and called his number. With few rings he picked her call.

"Yes Nila ma, works done?"

"Finished Mugilan, seems like you already met my dad. Where are you now?"

"Just roaming around near your campus, you can pick me near the gate in few minutes"

"Will be there, Bye"

She smiled at herself, talking with him is not like talking with a new person, it actually seems like talking with a well introduced person. Finding him near the gate, she stopped to pick him.

"How was your day Nila ma?"

"Went good, how was yours in the new city'

"Who told you I am new to this city?"

"You were here before?"

"Ya, for my official works visited Chennai few years before."

"Ok Ok,"

"Ok, Now where are we heading?"

"To my home, you want to go somewhere?"

"No, No, just continue."

Reaching the home, she asked him to enter in first. She washed her hands and legs in the front portion and entered in to find that his father is chatting with him. She entered the kitchen and made coffee for three. Joined them with some biscuits.

Seeing her, her father showed a happy smile. "You know what Mugil, she was roaming all gloomy for the past two weeks. Just not getting any information from you ate all her mind". She passed a glare at her father, making Mugilan smile at her. "I was really worried that something would have happened to him. But see him, sitting all fine and good in-front of me", she spoke looking at him. "I was in some works and thought of surprising her uncle, but in reverse your daughter surprised me this morning" his reply, made her to choke her coffee. "Daddy, why don't you take June to a walk." Hearing words of Nila, her father nodded his head understanding that something happened this morning. Leaving them alone, he took June for a walk.

"Don't take me wrong Mugilan, I don't want to worry him", as she spoke he gave an understanding nod. "Met your mom and dad?" she asked. "Ya, stayed with them for 2 days and informed them that I want to meet you. Started from there last night, coming here I took a hotel room and planned to meet you. Waited for you in your college entrance, seeing you coming inside, took a lift from a person came next to you. Thought of surprising you from behind, but you surprised me by giving me a warm hug" saying this he hugged the empty air in-front to him. She smiled at him.

"I already apologized for the same Mugilan, so tell me how are you?" as she asked, he moved to sit next to her. Held her hand into his, "Holding your hand and breathing the same air you breath, I am more than fine Nila ma". As he told, she nodded her head as smiled at him. "So now tell me how you know about my scar in right elbow?", She questioned him with a scrutinizing gaze at him. "Why don't you re-read our mail conversation, may be you yourself can find how". I remember every word we conversed.

"Ok then, tell me what you discussed after the phone conversation we made?", he asked. "Spoke about missing you and also worried about the hectic week" she answered sincerely remembering the things they discussed. "Only that dear Nila ma?!" he placed a question with a confidence that she missed something. "Just try to remember what you confessed to me in that mail, and you will yourself get to know how I know about your hurt." He spoke out very confidently and raised from his seat. She immediately got up from the place and moved to her system table. Passing a million-dollar smile, he too followed her. She opened her mail chains. The very first line of the mail stated that, *"Though it was not a long call, I feel like I recognize your voice somewhat.".* He slowly leaned on the computer table and confessed, "You remember my voice because you have already heard it. It means we already we met. To notify you the same, I stated in the next mail about your scar in right elbow, because." before he could complete the sentence, she spoke, "because you are the one who carried me and was asking me stay in conscious all the way to the hospital on that day" Her face was mixed with fear excitement and little confusion.

"Relax, Nila ma. I visited Chennai to pass on some confidential message to an important person here. I was never told that you are in Chennai. I think its fate that I met you on that day. In the local bus, I found you sitting opposite to me with bunch of kids and you were discussing about some moves in chess. As I saw you in your birthday photos, I somehow remembered you. When you got down in a bus stop, I started following in the curiosity that you may be person I was tied up with. But in the crowd I missed you in middle. Searching you randomly, I found you in mid of street collapsed in the pool of blood. All I decided is to save you, I was all nervous. Admitting you in the hospital, I thought of waiting till you get your conscious but my work schedule got changed and I was instructed to report immediately.

When I first received the mail from you, you mentioned as IIT Madras giving me the first hope that may be you are that girl I rescued. Then when you mentioned about training the kids in chess, I got it 80% confirmed. I just awaited to hear your voice and confirm it to 100%. When we chatted on that day, I was in cloud nine wondering how the plan of god works. When you too said that you remembered my voice, I was happy that you remember something about our very first meet."

All the time while he was narrating the events, Nila was wondering what is actually happening in her life. Everything really looked like a fairy tale for her.

"Thank you Mugilan for saving my life on that day. I really owe you one for that day." She said holding his hand into hers. "Don't you remember our gangs pledge, No Thank you and No Sorry", He said looking into her eyes.

Moving closer to her, his eyes were slowly soothing her raising heartbeat. "Can I hug you Nila ma?" His voice came out as a puppy request. She herself hugged him making him feel the all the emotions she was going through with.

After dinner, Mugilan informed that his mother planned to keep the official engagement in next month end on the birthday of his and her. He took a taxi and moved to his place of stay. She was just remembering every moments from the morning. Even after all these lovely moments, she felt something wrong around her. She gripped her gun which was kept under her pillow.

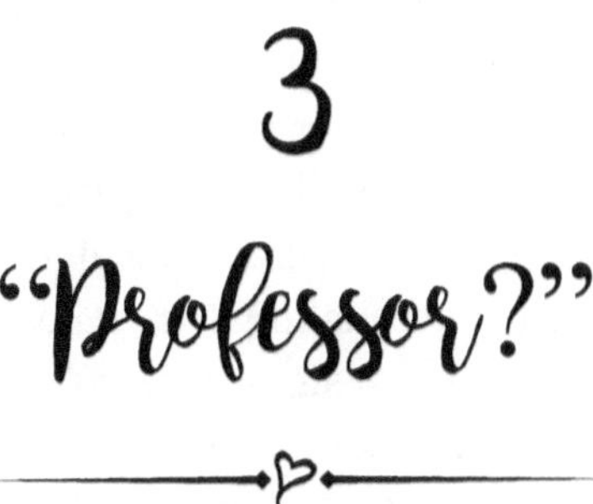

3

"Professor?"

Next day was a week end, Nila planned to visit her friends with Mugilan. She took her father's car and waited for Mugilan to finish the call he was having. When he got in, noticing something in her car's rear mirror Nila excused herself and went inside the house. After 5 minutes, she came back. When Mugilan questioned, she just gave a smile.

Nila received a call from her friend. Nila asked Mugilan to attend the call and make it in speaker. As soon as the call got attended her friend asked "Nila, Tea with biscuits or with sandwich". With a serious tone Nila answered, "I think biscuits dear. Moving in the traffic of race course road, hope all are there?", Opposite side just answered, "All ready" and the call got disconnected. Mugilan became more concerned seeing the nervous Nila. "Is everything ok Nila ma, she just asked a simple question, why are you so serious about it." Nila changed her frown face to a smiling one. "No Mugilan, nothing much. I am concerned about the timing we are going to reach there. I hate traffic. I need hustle free travel. I always be there on time. Today the plan got collapsed because of this traffic" Nila spoke giving a look with a rear mirror.

Mugilan placed his hands on her hands which was gripping the steering wheel. "Relax ma, Just few minutes. Traffic will be cleared. Just enjoy your moments with me. Don't think about anything else." She just held his hands into hers. She asked him to take a chocolate from her bag. He opened it and fed her making her smile. She asked him to take a bite. Crossing few signals, the car moved inside the parking lot of a café. Before getting down, Nila said, "Chocolate smearing in your cheeks, let me help you" Mugilan tried to see in the mirror. Nila resisted him from seeing the mirror and got a handkerchief from her purse. "Sorry Mugilan", Nila spoke cleaning his cheeks. "What's so serious to say sorry in this Nila ma" as he was asking. Nila just pressed that kerchief on his nose and held him strong. His conscious started to drop. "Nila, this is wrong. What's happening" he asked in his half mind. "Sorry Mugilan, just a small dose. Within one hour you will regain your conscious. Stay in car, Don't resist. Just sleep." All the thing Mugilan heard at the last was the bullet firing.

Nila was waiting next to Mugilan, her friend checked his pulse. "Nothing to worry Nila. He is fine. Don't worry.". "Anitha, all I am concerned now is, what to tell him when he wakes up.". "Just tell the truth Nila" said Aradhana who was nursing a deep cut on Nila's forehead. "I am not sure, what he is going to think about me. A liar, A murderer, ?!"Nila spoke with a disbelief. Anitha consoled her, "Don't think much. Just relax, let me go and see what Virushali and Jannvi is doing" As Anitha went, Aradhana discussed to Nila, "Who got the details about us? They traced till your address. There must be a head for these 5. Haven't got a chance to see anyone's face. As if we got time to remove their masks, forensic will give details in one hour, Let's wait Nila. As of now you enjoy your personal time with your police man. We will handle the things. We can't be roaming out from on. Just stay in the house. Will arrange the security", Aradhana was speaking, but stopped hearing moments from Mugilan.

"Mugilan, can you hear me? Drink some water." Nila assisted him to sit straight in the car seat. She gave some water. Drinking some water, he took a long breath. Without opening his eyes he asked, "What happened?". "Nothing much Mugilan, we can go to your room now. Let me explain you everything over there." Nila caressed his frowns on the forehead. He opened his eyes. His eyes showed horror seeing the bandage in her forehead. "What happened, can we go to the hospital.". "Will not be necessary Mr. Mugilan, I treated her wound. She is alright. And I am Aradhana. Sorry to have a first meet like this" Aradhana stretched her hands for a handshake. He responded to the handshake. "Is he awake" Anitha came towards them. "Yes, he is" said Aradhana leaving space for Anitha to see him. "Let me take a BP check, just to assure your dear lover." Anitha said taking out the BP reader eyeing the Nila whose cheeks are little red hearing her statement. "Sorry forgot to introduce, I am Anitha", Anitha added.

Within few minutes, Virushali and Jannvi joined the introduction meeting. Asking Mugilan to stay in the car, Nila came out to talk with her friends. "Aradhana, you go to the forensic and collect the details of the dead. Jannvi, noticed that one of them had a phone, just check the call logs and messages. Anitha arrange security for every one of our stay place also arrange a one for Mugilan's hotel. He will leave on Monday. Virushali, report the days happening with the Lexi sir. All 4 stay safe and be alert. Beware of strange happening around. I never wish to lose another one from my side." They all hugged Nila tight. Aradhana convinced Nila, "We will be safe, you just forget all these things and enjoy your time with your Police Man. It's time to accept that you are a human being Nila. Just grow that new found feelings for him." "I don't have any feelings for him Aradhana", as Nila said Anitha replied "I know you better Nila, just go. Give me a call once you reach the hotel and while leaving to home I will arrange an escort. Enjoy your time"

Coming to the driver seat, she locked her seat belt and saw Mugilan seeing her with billion questions. She is answerable to a one, who is ready to share his life with her.

Reaching the hotel, checking no one followed her she got down and opened the side door for Mugilan. Reaching the room, Mugilan was maintaining silence. Nila called the room service and asked for one coffee and one black coffee. Silence remained till the room service knocked the door. Getting the coffee in, she locked the door.

"Mugilan, just ask me whatever you wish to know", Nila started the conversation. "Very simple Nila, Truths. Simply Truth. Who are you actually? Who are those 4 girls I met few minutes before? Are you really a Professor? Mainly are you the one, who I was really engaged with?". Taking a deep breath, Nila begin to answer his questions. "Mugilan, I am the one who you got engaged with. I am the one mailed you. Only thing that was not revealed to you is, I am an undercover detective. Those 4 girls you met is my team. I am not a professor and but for spying a main suspect I am working as a Professor in the university. Please don't be mad at me, for hiding these things from you. I thought of introducing my team to you and reveal all these today. When I found an anonymous car standing there eying our house, I decided to give sedative for you and finish the business. I am sorry. I am really sorry. Only lie I told you was that I am a Professor. Other than that ever thing I told you was 100% true."

Hearing all her statements, Mugilan remained silent. Both their coffee cups became empty. "I can understand you Nila, I am leaving my family behind for their safety, but you are hiding your identity for the same reason. May I know about your mission?". Nila gave out a smile, "Keeping few things unknown is good Mugilan. I will take a leave now. There will be person near your door guarding you. Have a good sleep. Just text me the place wherever you go. Take care." Saying so, Nila got up from her place. "Just a minute Nila", Mugilan held her hands and took her near the cabinet. He took a gift parcel wrapped up in a red glitter cover. Giving her the gift he gave a side hug to her. "Take care Nila. I am highly concerned about your safety, Stay safe." Nila nodded her head and pressed a kiss on his hand. Bidding bye to him, she came out of his room and called Anitha.

Inside the room, Mugilan was seeing the hand where she kissed few minutes before. A little smile in his lips showed how much she matters to him.

Nila called Aradhana after reaching home. "I just need to run a finger print Aradhana, Collect the sample from me by tomorrow morning". "Whose fingerprints Nila ma, Are you ok?" Aradhana asked with a big concern. "It's Mugilan's finger print." Nila spoke eyeing the unopened gift box glittering RED.

4

"Why the hell do you suspect Mugilan on this Nila? I sincerely don't understand your point in this" Aradhana is yelling while the whole gang was seeing both Nila and Aradhana with a tensed look. "I don't trust anyone Aradhana. We were all hidden for past 2 years. But got exposed the very next day he visited. I am getting instincts that something is wrong around, since the morning I met him i.e. day before yesterday." Aradhana exhaled and just showed her hands up, "Just for few days Nila, please live for your feelings from your heart and not for the instincts from you bloody Brain. Please Nila, you deserve some happiness in your life. The day you visited his house and saw his room. I saw that glow in your face that day. You fell for him already Nila. Just your detective brain is clouding that. Propose him as you planned. Go on that date you have been planning for weeks. Trust me Nila, He is the one for you."

Nila's eyes welled up with tears, "Whatever you said is right. I got to know how much he loved this never met person from his room. I fell for him. I love him. But I don't want to lose anything from my side. I still couldn't give up on the lose we faced 3 years before. I remember his last words till now, "Nila, Save me. I have a family; I have a responsibility." I also remember how badly I failed him. He died in my arms Aradhana. Losing a best friend, a best team mate, is not an easy thing. I never want to lose anyone of you. Please just run those prints for me. Just for making sure."

Hearing her words, whole gang remembered the scene Nila spoke about. Anitha hugged Nila. "We will be careful Nila, but this day is yours. He is waiting for you in his room. Just go. Everything will be ok". Nila left Anitha from her hug and cleared her moistened eyes. "Just inform me the result Aradhana. I am leaving for now." Seeing the retreating figure of Nila, Jannvi said, "Run another background check for Mugilan.". "You too Janavi?" asked Virushali. "I always trust instincts of Nila, because they never go wrong".

Nila took her car, the guard of her drove the car. She kept on inhaling and exhaling in regular intervals. She tried to unplug her mind from her works. Reaching the hotel, she called him to come to parking lot. She asked the escort to follow them in another vehicle. As soon as he got into the car, Nila spoke out. "Sorry Mugilan, for spoiling your yesterday evening. But I promise to give you a wonderful day, today." As she spoke, he smiled at her. "Just promise me this thing Nila, No Works; No Guns; Strictly No Chloroform", as he said, she nodded with a guilt. "Past is past, from this moment it's just today and us. Nothing from yesterday, nothing about tomorrow", Nila said eying the road. "Mugilan nodded his head.

"So, where are we going today?", Mugilan asked. "That's a long list Mugilan, just wait and enjoy your day", Nila replied with a smile. "Okay, let's see what this Nila is planning for this Mugilan", Mugilan said holding her one hand which was on the gear.

First they visited a mall, as planned by Nila. Mugilan never left her hand. Just roaming through some random shops, suddenly a guy wearing a blue hat gave a red rose wrapped in a plastic shield to Mugilan. Mugilan got shocked. Nila asked him to receive the rose. He understood that she is planning something. He got the rose with a smile. They roamed the three floors and he received two more roses in next floors from person's wearing blue hats.

Next they went to have some Brunch, and there he got a rose. Then visited Aquarium, Pet Shop and a Nursery. Every place they visited Mugilan received a rose. He was smiling all the time. Nila was just witnessing beautiful moments of her life. They had lunch in a hotel and ice-cream in a road side shop. They chatted all along the travel, about each other's school life, college life, training period etc. At last around 4.00 PM, Nila parked her car in one end of Marina beach. The surprise continued, he started receiving a rose whenever crossing a statue along the side road of beach. Helping him, Nila collected the rose and kept it in a jute bag. They sat at one point and started to watch the waves.

Nila's watch made a beep sound, saying that it is 6.00 PM. "So, have you counted how many roses you have received from morning." Nila asked eyeing the last two roses he received few minutes ago. Mugilan raised his eyebrows and said, "I think it's 27 roses, representing our 27 years on this earth under the same sky." Nila gave an amused smile, saying that she is impressed. "The surprise is hidden in every single rose you received from morning.", Nila said. Hearing her Mugilan immediately saw the rose packed in a plastic shield. Looking more deep, he found there is a paper cutting in the stem of every rose he received. "Now your work is to collect all the papers and arrange them to get that secret message I am trying to convey you from this morning. I have an important call to attend. You just try to finish the task and call me. I called the escort to park there. You can sit inside the car and do your puzzle solving. Take care." She waved a bye and left from there.

Mugilan was much thrilled to solve the puzzle. As soon as the car came, he hoped in and started to remove the clues from every roses. Checking the clues, he had an idea that it should be a photo. He was all into the puzzle, forgetting his surroundings.

Nila called Aradhana. "Just give me the straight answer Aradhana.". "I have no idea of hiding things from you Nila. He is clean. His work and everything he is clean. You can just keep your pistol back in the car and continue the surprise", As Aradhana said, Nila touched the pistol which was safely hiding under her over-jacket. "Have a great night ahead Nila , Bye." Aradhana disconnected the call.

Nila drank some water given by her escort. She instructed him few things and started to move towards the car. She found a 2 year who was completely immersed in arranging the 27 pieces of a photo. "Need a hand, Mugil?", as Nila asked, Mugilan not removing his eyes from the papers, "Just 16 pieces, the picture will be a complete one. I already have guess what the photo is about." "Ok, will be waiting for you. Come out once done.", saying so Nila hid the gun in-front of the car and came out to receive the chill breeze of the beach.

Mugilan placed the last piece of the photo in the correct place. The smile in his face grew bigger. The photo is captured from his room back in hometown. The photo of the painting Mugilan made on his room wall. Beautifully drawn Moon hiding its half behind the clouds9. With the wording "I love you Nila" below the drawing. So, visiting for his mothers birthday is not a general visit but also background check on him. Mugilan chuckled on her little actions.

Coming out of the car, he found Nila standing there watching the Moon. All he thought to do is hug her from behind. He slowly moved towards her and hugged from behind. Though she flinched first, seeing him behind her nerves eased. Some minutes dissolved with the rushing sound of the waves and the high wind. "I couldn't believe that how you fall in love with me even before meeting me." Nila spoke out first. "Who said Nila, I never met you. Every time I watch the night sky, you were there. My Moon (Nila) was there, playing with clouds (Mugil). You were always there in my embrace every night.", Mugilan answered just eyeing the Moon which was slowly rising high on the sky. Nila adjusted herself in his arms in a way seeing his face. There was only Love in those eyes. She really missed being with this man. She should have known about him before years and years. She wished to get all those lone years, with him again. "Which is the moment you fell for me Mugil? ", Nila asked. "There is no exact moment when the earth, sky, moon is formed Nila ma, but it is real and solid. My love for you is just like that." Hearing his statement, Nila just stood in his toes and kissed his left cheek. Turning her towards the sea, he kissed her left cheek and spoke, "Just see that Moon Nila, it grows and becomes full. Then it diminishes and become invisible. But it's for the eyes of the people on earth. But think for the cloud which moves around the Moon. For it, the Moon is always the full moon. Just like that, you were always that full moon for me. For all the eternity I get to embrace this full moon. Love you Nila." As he confessed, Nila turned and hugged him tight. She hasn't spoken anything, but her grip on him remained tight. "It's getting cold Nila, Let's go to the room.", as Mugilan said, she left him and adjusted herself to the reality. "Father asked us to join with him for dinner, can we go to my home?" As

Nila asked Mugilan nodded and said, "Let me make a call to the travel agency about my flight tomorrow and we can leave.". saying so he took his phone from his pant pocket, accidently a small cover fell from his pockets. It went unnoticed by both Nila and Mugilan, but a pair of eyes watched this.

5

"Bullets"

Tomorrow is a big day of her life, her engagement. But the nervousness in her face said that she is not happily welcoming the big day. Aradhana repeated the same thing umpteenth time, "Nila, they would have opted different transport. Stay Calm". Nila was in no mood to hear this.

She started to get the bad instincts again, there developed a pounds of fear in her stomach pit. Last time, when he visited, they faced a threat. Now again he is visiting and she is getting the same bad instincts. There is something unknown bad around him. She loves him, loves him a lot. Still she couldn't avoid the thinking.

They heard the car honk and Aradhana looked out to find a car entering in. Aradhana came out with Virushali to find that it is Mugilan who was getting down from the car. Before Aradhana tried to call Nila out, she herself came out following them. Seeing Mugilan, she let out a long breath. She greeted his parents and Nila's Father invited them in. Mugilan's mother took Nila's hand into her's, "I really missed you da Nila ma, my idiot son got up with some works in last minute and we missed the flight. Later booked another one and landed this late. Sorry for the delay da.". "Don't be sorry ma, its ok. You will be very tiered, please freshen up and let have the dinner. I have arranged a room for you to stay. Vishnu anna take the bags to the room we cleaned today", Nila instructed the temporary worker she hired.

Everyone entered in, except for Mugilan who was helping Vishnu for unloading the luggage and our angry bird Nila. Aradhana was praying all the gods that Mugilan should not have any black eye. Mugilan paid the car and the car left. It was only Nila and Mugilan now. "Sorry Nila ma, I was suddenly ordered to meet someone regarding my next assignment. Don't keep this red chili nose. Sorry ma.", As Mugilan was speaking, Nila left him and entered in the house. Nila doesn't want to vent out her anger on him. Mugilan just followed her in. Nila's father was speaking something to his best friend, stood up to make space for Mugilan to sit. Mugilan sat next to Nila's dad, still eying the angry Nila.

After dinner, everyone left to sleep after discussing tomorrow ceremony's time and details. It was planned to keep the engagement ceremony at evening and at morning they planned to visit few temples in local. Nila entered in, sending off Aradhana and Virushali. Night lamp was giving 10% of light. Nila got terrified with someone hugging her from behind. Got relaxed with his voice. "Sorry Nila ma, haven't done on purpose". Nila struggled to leave from his hold. "First leave me Mugil, I am in no mood to talk with you"

He just lifted her in his arms, she just stayed silent. Made her to sit comfortably in her bed, he locked the door. "See Nila, please try to understand." He pleaded. "I accept, you got works. Everyone gets work. But haven't you got time to call me to inform that you are taking different flight. Not even a call is must, just a message was enough. Do you know the present condition around me? we are being informed that a gang has already got the information about what we are searching. We are already asked to keep very low profile and asked to guard our loved ones. Do you know how many bad things ran in my mind? How many blood drenched scenes crossed my mind? Any idea, how many gods I have been praying the whole day? Never just say a..." Her remaining rants were eaten by the kiss Mugilan placed on the corner of her lips.

Placing his head on her lap, Mugilan spoke "I really haven't thought this much da Nila ma, I thought just 7 hours of delay, haven't thought all these scenarios. I promise this will be the last time I am behaving this careless. I will keep myself informed. Please never keep your face that grumpy and angry." "Just inform me things Mugil, I expect nothing much. My condition is getting critical over here. We just need a week or less to finish the mission. We are very near, but I am having a bad instinct that something is going very wrong. I am already fighting things inside Mugil, I even thought of canceling the engagement. My team convinced me to keep things normal, so we can continue working underground." As Nila spoke all serious, Mugilan sat next to her taking her head on his shoulders.

"Everything will be fine soon. Just remember we are having a big day tomorrow. It looks like My mom decided a marriage date. Hope she will reveal tomorrow to us. Concentrate on your pity lover here. My wait for you is not just days and months, Its years and years Nila ma. Just don't let your profession spoil our personal bubble" Nila nodded her head and placed a kiss on his cheeks. After wishing each other Good night, Mugilan left to his room.

When Nila tried to get some sleep, her phone ringed. It's from Aradhana. "Nila, traced the exact location, we can break in now. Will pick you up in minutes. Don't forget to take the needed ones". Call got disconnected. Nila dressed up and took a small brief case which was hidden in a secret compartment of her room. She slowly sneaked out of her house. Took a chocolate and started to have some small bites out of it. A car came by and she hoped in.

"Are you sure Anitha, we traced the correct location?" Jannvi asked looking at the tab screen showing up the location. "Leave the technology, decoding etc. think about the day Doctor spoke with us. He said, he is in his best friend's place and also stated that he visited him on an important note. Two days after that, he was found dead. After all these years of research, we know for sure only friend Doctor had was Shankardev. Unfortunately, we found that he too was killed brutally after a week of Doctors death. But we never guessed the hiding place would be Shankardev's house. But in the journals of Doctor we stole from the university with the help of Nila, it was mentioned in codes. When decoded, it clearly gave a latitude and longitude leading to Shankardev's house. Logically and technically I am 100% sure that the place is Shankardev's house." As Anitha finished, Nila added "Only challenging thing is, we have to find where it was hidden in that two floor building, we have to finish the search before the sun rises. It's an abandoned building for past few years, we should not grab any attention from the public around." All other 4 nodded their heads.

They entered through the back side walls. Opened the back side door, leading them into the house. Using the help of their head lights, they decided to split up and search. Nila & Aradhana moved to first floor. Hours passes, they all felt like searching a needle fell on the hay bush.

Nila tried to think in a way Doctor used to think. He is a sentimental fool, he always tells goddess Saraswathi and Lakshmi should always be kept higher from the grounds. He used to keep all his notes and samples on the top most shelf, as he is short he used to keep a stool around the lab. Its somewhere higher, higher. Nila started to think about the day he spoke from his friend's place. She remembered hearing the gush of air flowing through the speakers while he was speaking. "Terrace", Nila spelled. She started to move towards the stairs, gaining the attention of Aradhana who was searching in room near the stairs. Seeing Aradhana coming out, Nila signaled her to follow. Terrace was locked, using the silencer Aradhana fired the lock. There stood a room with a glass ceiling. It exactly looked like a storage room, which is the perfect place to hide things.

When tried to open the door, it was locked too. Another bullet. All the things were covered with dust, Nila coughed twice. Aradhana started to search with Nila, there was a big wooden cabinet standing there in the corner of the room. There was also a small stool at the foot of the cabinet confirming the theory of Nila. Nila opened the cabinet, it was empty, expect the fifth last shelf. There was a blue color safe, safe of the Doctor. They have been searching this for the past years. They both got a smile.

Before they tried to open the safe, they heard some footsteps. "Must be our guys", Aradhana said and moved towards the door. Thud! Nila turned to see Aradhana on the floor with blood all over her.

6

Nila took her gun out. Before she could blink, a bullet teared her left arm muscle. she has no time to think further. Two masked men entered in, she shot them and came out. Took the other brief case she bought from her house from the grip of Aradhana. She had no time to check the pulse of Aradhana, more foot sounds are approaching.

Checking around, she found the near buildings terrace with minimum distance. Just threw the brief cases to the next building and she too jumped. She hasn't stopped, started to jump from one terrace to the next near gripping the brief cases safely. She heard some bullets are firing in her direction. Finally hid under roof when she felt she was not chased anymore. Took her phone, called Vishnu, the temporary worker of her house. "Vishnu, sending my GPS location, pick me up. Don't need to inform the head office. Come alone, bring your gun". Vishnu though terrified with the voice of Nila, acted immediately.

Nila, checked her wound, Bullet is struck in her muscle and all her jumping's made the hurt worse. Her broken watch showed the time around 4.00. She heard some siren sounds, definitely the bullet firing would have pulled the night patrol towards the area. She slowly checked the ways to get of the building. She found the roofing was little low and jumping on the roof will help her to land on the road.

It has risks, but she has to take this risk. She jumped and crash landed on the road, making sure nobody noticed her she started to walk. Vishnu called her and she gave some landmark. Her hand pained a lot.

As soon as Vishnu came Nila guided him towards their safe house, where they meet officially. Nobody knows this house. The door got opened with her thumb scanning and retina scanning. She lost little blood and she was losing her conscious slowly. But the mission in her mind made her to move towards the secret basement room hiding below the tea table.

Vishnu who was standing out was really worried about Nila. But no-body can act against the words of Nila. Nila hid both the brief cases carefully. She again came up and locked the door and hid the door with mattress. Came out and locked the main door. Coming to Vishnu she gave a paper to him, she spoke, "Send the local police to this address, Team is there. I am not sure." She fell down unconscious before finishing her sentence. Vishnu got panicked, called the emergency ambulance.

With the CBI id of Vishnu, Hospital took Nila for the operation room. The bullet was removed and due to the blood loss, she stayed in the unconscious state. Nearly at morning 7.00 AM, she regained her conscious. Doctor checked her and asked the nurse to change her to normal ward. Vishnu was waiting for her. "Team was not there mam, not in the address you gave me.", Nila got shocked and got up from her bed. "They must be there, call the inspector who went there. I want to talk with him right now." She removed the trips from her hand. Her left hand pained a little. "Finish the discharge formalities soon Vishnu, we have to visit the Shankardev's house". Vishnu nodded his head and left. Nila closed her eyes. Her past years ran in front of her. Aradhana's figure covered with blood disturbed her. Her eyes welled up. She wants to cry aloud, but she controlled. It's not time to be emotional. She has to stay strong, she has to find her team.

Vishnu came with discharge papers and Nila came out. Vishnu called someone to bring a car. Within minutes' car came and Vishnu took the driving seat and Nila sat in front with him. She started to guide him the way. In the way the police who checked Shankardev's house called Nila. "Sir, can you please be brief about what you saw there in the house address I gave.". "Mam, we found nothing unusual. The house was locked. When we entered in, we found the house full of dust and spider webs. We checked all two floors and the terrace. There were no forced entry or dead bodies. Everything was usual mam." Nila replied a Thank you and disconnected the call. "Something is wrong Vishnu, I haven't mentioned anything about forced entry or dead body, but the police officer is mentioning it. Have you mentioned any?" "No mam, I just asked them to check the spot for any suspects", Vishnu replied confidently. "Some one more powerful is influencing the local police department." Nila said closing her eyes tightly. "What can we do now mam?", Vishnu asked parking the car aside. "Let's get the keys from the local police station and check things from our side."

Opening the house, she got shocked to see everything on the same place how she saw that while entering through back door. She saw the back door, it looked as an old lock which was devoid from opening for years. Climbed up to terrace and found that it was locked, she found the key in the bunch she collected from the police station. She found the storage room locked too, opening it, no trace of Aradhana. She felt like her whole world collapsed. She fainted.

When she opened her eyes, Mugilan was sitting near her bed. She looked around and found that it's her room. Before she tried to speak, Mugilan kept his pam on her lips, asking her to be silent. "Happy Birthday Nila, From this birthday you are never gonna be alone without me. Weak, strong, Happy, sad, up, down, whatever you become and whatever the situation becomes, I will never leave your side. Will always be there with you Nila, Love you so much." As Mugilan finished, small tears made a way from her eyes. He wiped her tears. She sat up with the help of him. "Sorry Mugilan, some unexpected vents turned out. Just give me the day, will be back at the engagement ceremony on the time of the event. I have to leave now." She spoke turning her heart back to the promise she made for her profession. "You can leave Nila, Vishnu and some other officials are waiting for you in front." Mugilan said hiding his disappointment.

Nila checked her hurt, it was painful, she wore her over jacket hiding the maximum of the bandages under it. She took a long breath and moved towards the door. Her works are saved, but she lost her team, which loved her believed her and mainly she lost the people who kept their highest hopes on her. All she now has in her hands is this man standing near her bed, with unconfessed feelings for her.

She turned towards him and took his hands into her, "I promise you Mugil, I will return back to your arms at least at the last pounding of my heart." His eyes let out the tears he was holding back, seeing her that vulnerable in hands of Vishnu, nearly shook his life, but he stayed calm just to may her comfortable. Unable to control himself more, he pressed his lips on her, assuring again he is there to make her heart beat even if gets stopped.

With all the mixed emotions, Mugilan and Nila exchanged the rings in-front of the elders in the temple nearer. Dinner was arranged for the people came to bless the couples. Nila was spreading smiles at everyone showing that she is happy. From the side of Mugilan knows well that she is doing this to keep the elders happy. He knows she is faking everything. Still he waited until they reach their home. Around night 9.30 they reached the home and everyone went to rest.

Mugilan changed his dress and came out to see the fully dressed Nila loading her gun. "I am leaving Mugilan, just inform daddy that I will return within this week end. I have mailed him the college details where I am going for the symposium. Please save my secret. Let him think I am at peace." Mugilan nodded his head. She hugged him. Having him in her arms gave her a strength and reason to comeback. "Will call you once things get normal." She said and walked out through front door.

Waving a bye to Mugilan, Nila got into the car taking a deep breath. She knows this could be the last bye she said to him. She is moving towards the Yelagiri hills, where the antonyms call guided her She knows for sure the person who spoke haven't called to inform the place of her friends but a trap. It is the call from that bloody scoundrels who took her team from her. She is not going in the hope that they 4 are alive, but she wants a respectful funeral for them the least thing She can do for her friends. Her head office rejected her request to rescue her team as Nila was not sure if they are alive. Her head Lexi gave an unofficial approval and provided the needed arms and two men for the rescue operation.

Vishnu sitting next to Nila asked her, "Mam, are you sure it was the tip call to find our team ?". Nila gave a smile, "Vishnu, I know. I am walking towards by death grave. I know it's a trap. Still I don't want to lose the last chance I have in my hand finding them." Vishnu stayed silent.

They are just 2 Km away from the co-ordinates the call mentioned. They decided to hide the vehicle and go by foot. It already started getting dark. Nila insisted Rachel to stay behind in the car and asked him return back to Chennai If he doesn't any information from her for next 4 hours. Walking towards the destination, Nila spoke to Vishnu, "Vishnu, you should never come to rescue me. All your duty is to watch for the team and if you are not finding any, you should retreat back immediately." Vishnu said immediately, "No mam, I can't leave you alone. I am coming with you. If something happens, I will be there taking you back." Nila in her rude tone spoke, "It's my order Vishnu. No more discussion on this". Vishnu nodded his head.

They found smoke raising in sky from somewhere near, they walked towards the smoke and found a small building. The co-ordinates matched the direction of the house. When tried walking near, they found the house was guarded by two armed men. She can take down the two men but not sure how many are around there. She asked Vishnu to stay down and she advanced in-front. Assembling the silencer in her gun, Nila took the two guards down. Entering in the house, Nila found the house empty except the wooden box at the corner of the house. When she opened the box she found a white paper folded. The paper read, "Welcome Nila".

She expected this welcome, but not the sharp pain on her left shoulder. She started to retreat back from the house. She has to warn Vishnu; she is going to lose her conscious. She came out, tried to keep her eyes open. With four to five step forward, slowly her vision started to blur. She fell down.

Opening her eyes, she couldn't identify anything around her. It was full of dark. Time should be past 12. When trying to move, she found her hands and legs are tied to a chair. She shouted, "Anybody here?". No reply. Her voice echoed. She stayed calm and tried to relax her mind. She knows what is coming for her. They got her to get the information about the location of the doctors safe she is hiding. She hasn't told the department that she recovered the same. She doubted that someone in the department is in favor of the men who attacked them on that night.

After a wait of few hours, the dim light in the corner of that room glowed. She remembered, this is the house where she found the welcome note. She is tied as her back facing the door. She heard the footsteps around her. Door opened. "Hello Nila", a familiar voice came behind her. "Noooo" her mind cried. She desperately wanted to prove that the owner of the voice behind is not "Mugilan".

He is standing in front of her. Everytime his eyes showered care and love, but today all his eyes carry was evilness. She tried to gather her words, all she was able to say was, "Mu". Her voice trembled. "Give her some water Hari", he ordered someone standing behind her. Mugilan removed the tape from her right hand, but she hasn't moved her hand a bit.

After drinking some water, Hari pulled her hands and taped again to the chair. Nila hasn't protested or resisted. Her mind got blocked. She expected some betrayal. But not from Mugilan. So her instincts were right. She cursed herself for not taking her intuition more serious. How is this possible. How is this even possible. With all these thoughts struggling in her mind, her conscious slowly slipped.

This time when she woke up, Mugilan was sitting opposite to her with that smirk in his face. "Had a good sleep it seems Nila ma?". She maintained her silence. She made herself in a state of battle between her heart and mind. Her heart was bargaining that all the moment she had with this evil eyed man was true. But her mind pinpointed her intuitions from her first meeting with him. Closing her eyes tight, tears made its way down taking her hopes down. "Wow Nila, I heard that no one can break you.

I think the credit goes to my acting", Mugilan's voice made her open the eyes to witness that evil eyes again. His right hand finger still carried the ring she gave him. Her mind slapped her with the purpose. She started to collect herself back. Whatever happened between Mugilan and her, is love from her side. If he cheated her blame is not on her feelings. Now priority is her friends. She voiced out, "Where are my team mates Mugilan!". "Ha ha ha, two mistakes in one sentence, First I don't know where your team mates are, when my guys attacked you on that day someone helped your team mates and they escaped from us. I don't care about their whereabouts. Second mistake is I am not Mugilan, I am Aravindan. Just a plastic surgery. See no difference. Now all you have to do is inform us where you hid the doctors safe. You have 12 hrs. time or else I will take the honor of sending your father and Mugilan's parents to where I sent Mugilan" saying the last line he laughed aloud making Nila anger. Aravindan left speaking all these. Nila was left alone with a guard behind her. All she got to see is the empty wall in-front of her, also an empty life ahead. 12 hrs. what can she do. Nila closed her eyes. Helped herself to gather the information Mugilan who turns out to be Aravindan conveyed her in last few minutes. Her friends are not in the hands of this gang, He killed Mugilan and replaced in his place, her family's life is in danger now.

Few things confused her. When she checked his finger prints when they met first, matched with Mugilan so Aravindan got replaced after that visit. It should have happened in his hometown. But how she hasn't found any difference, her head got heavy. She has to find a way out of this House. If she resists to inform them the details they need, everyone she values more in her life will be moved to danger. What is she going to do? What can she do?

Mugilan entered in with that boy Hari. Hari removed her right hand tape. Another one placed a stool infront of her with food plate on it. "it's been more than 12hrs you had some food, eat" Aravindan said and Nila said, "I have important works out Mug., Sorry Aravindan, I have to find my team. You can't reach the doctors safe without me. Take me to the address I give you. Will help you to get that doctors safe. But you have to promise me that you will release me". "Are you planning to escape Nila" Aravindan asked. "No, I have to rescue my team. I am willing to give up on my mission as the cost. Believe me" Nila said with a pleading tone.

Car started to move forward, Nila was sitting between Hari and Aravindan with her hands tied tight. Thinking about something Nila started the conversation. "Aravindan, Do you know what is there in Doctor's safe?", as Nila asked Aravindan let out a laugh. "That's not my business Nila, I got orders to take the doctors safe once you find the same. One Idiot interrupted my plan. If things went good, I would have received my 10 crores by now. I will kill that scoundrel if I lay my hands on him." Nila remained silent. Few minutes later again she asked, "What you did with Mugilan?". Aravindan showed his fingers on his neck and sliced it, enacting he killed Mugilan by cutting his throat. Nila's eyes brimmed with tears. She tried to blink off the tears. Aravindan seeing her spoke out, "He hid only one thing from you and I took advantage of it. He had a calcium deficiency and he was taking calcium tablets regularly and I exchanged those tablets with a sedative. It helped me to abduct him and finish him off. It was really easy to fool you and his parents. No one found out the difference between us. All credits to my plastic surgeon."

He kept on speaking, hurting Nila. She couldn't accept the fact that Mugilan is no more. She prayed for her team mates. She prayed God to at least give her friends back. She started to think about her escape plan. She has 0% idea to return the Doctors safe. If someone bad lays hands on that, there is no guarantee for the future of the country. The safe contains things that may start a war.

They reached the safe house where Nila hid the safe. She spoke, "only one can enter with me inside, decide who comes along with me inside". Hari volunteered to go with Nila. Aravindan protested, "No, I will handle this. If I don't come out in half an hour just finish her father." Nila took a deep breath and moved to the door with Aravindan following her behind close. She still couldn't accept that it is not Mugilan, his closeness reminded their first hug. Pushing herself out of her emotional thing, she opened the door with her retina and thumb scanning. As soon as they both entered in, Nila closed the door and did something with the door access. Aravindan was busy with his phone missing her work with the door access.

"Aravindan, I know you are just a bullet from someone's gun. You are not looking that bad guy. I am not sure how much you are good in science but I hope you can understand some basics with my explanation." Nila stopped waiting for the reaction from Aravindan. He nodded asking her to continue.

"The drug in the doctor's safe is the experiment regarding all the virus that affect the human's health. Instead many vaccines we take against many viruses, doctor planned to give a one vaccination that could oppose all the virus. He successfully created the same, but when it was tested it resulted in causing over aging. According to the doctor if a person takes the vaccine at age of 25, with 2 years he will become old like a 50 years' man. So doctor decided not to proceed with the medicine and destroyed all the samples he created. But for the future reference he hid one dose of drug and the formulas and methods he used to create the same. A person who worked as assistant with the doctor got to know about this and informed doctor's son regarding this. Doctors son who was money minded thought of selling it to the opposite country so that they can start a Bio war on us. We were on the doctor's security team during this problem. When doctor refused to give the drug, His son cruelly made an attack on doctor's laboratory and we lost one of our team mate in that. After few months, everything became normal and we thought doctor's son gave up. But unfortunately doctor got killed." Nila gave a pause and checked her watch and continued.

"If this falls in a wrong hand Aravindan we all will be equally affected. Please move back from this evil project. Let me destroy the last dose and formulas Doctor saved. Please Aravindan, I will help you to erase any case on you and delete all your trace in this case. Please Aravindan." Nila pleaded.

"Nila, what is the name of your doctor?" Aravindan asked looking at Nila. "His name is Dr. Sathyamoorthy Katkur", Nila answered him thinking why he is asking such a question after she explained all these. "And do you know my full name Nila?", Aravindan asked taking steps towards her. "No" Nila replied with the fear raising in her heart. "My name is Aravindan Sathyamoorthy Katkur, for your kind information, I am the one who killed one of your team mate years back." Nila's heart skipped a beat.

9

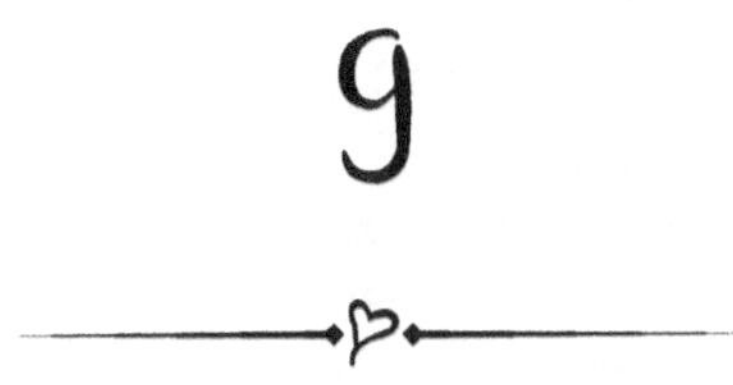

Blood was oozing from the corner of Nila's lips. Her left hand was broken. Aravindan was sitting in the sofa with his blood on his forehead and his right cheek showed a deep cut. Nila was unconscious. Aravindan tried opening the main door but no use, it was locked. It was bullet proofed and kinetic repulsive. He found his phone broken beyond repair in the fight they had few minutes before. The glass frame Nila used made a deep hurt on his cheeks. He searched the whole house for the safe but no luck. Nila murmured something in her half-conscious. "Nila, tell me where you hid the safe. Your family is in danger. They would have killed your family by now. Wake up you bloody girl." Aravindan shouted in dismay. Nila gained her conscious and let out a laugh making Aravindan angrier.

Nila wiped the blood from her mouth and spoke, "The moment I entered the house, I locked the house with the emergency code. Which will automatically alert my department and my father. He would have taken Mugilan's family and himself into a safe house. I received the safe signal from my father just minutes before your confession on your identity. You are not leaving this house and you can never have your hands on your fathers safe." "Nila, I warn you open the main door. Enough of your plans. I am going to kill you in 5 minutes if you ae not opening the door." Aravindan barked like a dog at Nila.

Nila stood up holding her left hand in her right. "You know why your father never allowed you into his experiments. It's because you are a stupid. I locked the door with the emergency code. Only my team mates can open the door from outside. No one can barge in through this house and no one can jump out of this house without my concern." As Nila spoke, Aravindan tried to raise his hand to slap Nila, Nila got his fingers in air and twisted it. He cried in pain, she broke his fingers in a second. Before he could think more, she broke another glass vase in his head making him unconscious.

Without wasting time, Nila helped herself to relocate her left hand bone. It pained much but she fixed it. Carried Aravindan to a chair and locked his hands with the chair's arm rest and tied his legs together. Taking a first aid box from their belongings, she treated her wounds. Made a bandage to her left hand. Injected Mugilan with an injection which will help him to sleep for few hours. Sat on the sofa and rested her back bone to the comfort. Slowly she started to cry. She lost her Mugilan, the one who loved her so much even before meeting her. The one who showed love is not by looks or expectations. She cried out all the pain she was holding for the past hours. How is she going to face Mugilan's family now? How the parents who took six to seven months of missing a big deal, going to deal the fact that he is missing for the rest of their lives? She cried her heart out.

After a good one hour of crying, something strikes Nila's mind. Who helped her team in Shankardev's house? There are two possibilities; One, someone willing to help her saved them and keeping them undercover; Otherwise someone who wants revenge from her took them and keeping them undercover. She dozed off on the sofa.

Hearing muffled moaning from Aravindan, Nila woke up from her slumber. She adjusted herself and checked him. He was trying to adjust his eyesight. "Nila dragged a chair and made herself sit right in-front of him with 6 to 7 feet distance between them. Aravindan tried to remove the ties from his hand. "Sorry Aravindan, you are struck with me here. I have few questions, just answer me." As soon as Nila spoke, Aravindan gritted his teeth. Nila laughed seeing his raising anger. "No", he shouted. "Ok, then I am making a coffee for myself. Hope you don't mind" Nila stood from her place and moved to kitchen. When she returned with a coffee mug in her hands, Mugilan was ready to answer. "Ask your questions Nila". She sat in her place and started her question, "Exactly from when are you following us?". "From the day one of the mission I have been following you. Just few days before Mugilan's arrival I found that you got the doctors journal from the university. I informed the people who showed interest on my father's invention. They were so determined to get the drug, so I got the fixed money 50 crores as advance and will get the remaining 50 once I handover the drug." Aravindan spoke with hint of greediness in his voice. Nila asked her next question, "Who plotted this plan of abducting Mugilan and you replacing him?". "It's idea of the head person from the opposite country. They somehow traced your mail and found about your relation with Mugilan. They asked me to follow you and Mugilan from the moment he landed in Chennai. I was thinking a way to take Mugilan down from the picture. I found his calcium tablets which fell from his pockets on the day you proposed him in beach. That helped to plan against him, I replaced him in his hometown after watching his schedules for few days." Hearing Aravindan's statement Nila started to feel tears on her cheeks. She lost Mugilan because of her profession. Composing herself to normal, she posted the next question. "Do you know the whereabouts of the Head person you ae speaking, are they in India or just guiding you from their country?". "They will kill me, If I reply this question. Please leave me. I will erase all my identity and leave the country, because either way I don't have security for my life. I will give you how much money you demand" As Aravindan spoke, Nila broke her coffee mug on his head. "You are testing my patience Aravindan. I am not sweet as I look. After all the things you did with my Mugilan, how you imagined that I will leave you. I will rip your soul apart." Nila said giving two to three slaps tearing his cheek muscles. "He is my first love Aravindan. He proved me the love at first sight. He showed me there is something beyond work is not a mistake but a needed one. I remember every words of his diary he wrote from his college times, how much he loved me, how much he waited for me to enter his life as his love. You just not killed a person there for money, you killed two. Even now, as you have his face, what I am giving you is very less compared to one I have in my mind" Nila raised her hand to punch him, but before she could do that, the main door flung open. It was Aradhana. Seeing Aravindan tied to chair. She ordered Anitha who followed her and entered next, "Anitha tie his eyes and put him in the basement. Seeing them in-front of her eyes, made Nila to loose last string of emotional strength she was holding.

10

Nila kneeled down thanking all the gods who saved her friends. Anitha tied his eyes and removed something from his ears. Aravindan was in half conscious tried to speak something, Anitha closed his mouth restraining him from speaking. She with the help of Jannvi carried him to the basement. Anitha treated his wounds and gave him painkillers. Within half an hour they joined the weeping Nila and consoling Aradhana in the living room. Virushali came from the kitchen with three bowls of instant noodles.

Aradhana fed Nila the noodles and other three shared the bowls. Nila lied down in sofa and eventually slept. The four without making any noise moved to the bedroom with the electronic device they removed from the ears of Aravindan. Virushali dismantled the device and took the transmitter out and started to search the receiving point. Within few minutes they found the receiver's location. Jannvi and Aradhana decided to go and finish off the receiving point. Jannvi took the transmitter with her.

As they left, Anitha said "They planned everything perfectly, they trusted no body it seems". "The one with guilt never accept the opposite innocent Anitha ma" said Virushali clearing the vase pieces and glass pieces from the floor. They both started to clean the hall without any noise as Nila was sleeping on the sofa. They too felt tiered and decided to sleep in bedroom in the idea that Nila will sleep for more 2 hrs. But Nila woke up within half an hour. The moment she woke up all her mind reminded her was the revenge she wished to get. She moved to the basement.

Aravindan was sleeping on the coach in the basement with trips running down his nerves. This made her angry. Who is he? A guest or a victim but a cold blooded murderer who killed her Mugilan. She filled a water tub, removed his trips and dragged him to the tub and dug his face inside the tub. This made Aravindan gain conscious in spite of the painkiller doses. He slowly murmured, "Nila ma..." Hearing that Nila got angrier, how the hell can he call her with the word how her Mugilan calls her. She gave a tight slap to him, pulling him to the reality. He couldn't see who was there in-front of him as the black bind fold resisted him from seeing. "Nila ma, just hear me what I am trying to say." As he spoke, Nila kicked him on his stomach. "Never use that tone on me, are you trying to act like Mugilan and escape from me. I really appreciate your acting skills. I myself wanted to believe that you are Mugilan. Every time I touch you I feel my Mugilan, but it's all my stupid emotions." Moving to the culinary set she took a knife and came down again.

Entering in, all she saw was the blood drenched Mugilan. Nila fell down on her knees. She couldn't control herself, From the first she is fighting inside if he is her Mugilan or Aravindan? But if he was Mugilan he would have confessed the truth once we came into the house alone, he continued to behave Aravindan. "Ahhhhhhh", Nila shouted, waking up Virushali and Anitha. They both rushed down not finding her in the sofa. He still under the influence of pain was murmuring "Nila ma". It raised her anger and she was moved to him. Throwing the knife away, she raised her hand to punch his mouth.

"Nila stop it" Anitha shouted rushing inside the basement. She hugged Nila from behind and dragged her behind towards the stairs leading to upstairs. Virushali started to dress up the wounds of him. The moment Nila reached the upstairs, she fainted in the hands of Anitha. Her mind couldn't take up more stress. Her mind and heart playing this Mugilan or Aravindan card for a long time.

"We need Aradhana here before she wakes up next. I gave her a small dose of sleeping pill which will keep her down for next 2 hrs. Call Aradhana. What is the condition of him down there?" asked Anitha "I should call it worse, drenched in water and blood. I think he needs an immediate hospital administration. I called Vishnu to take an ambulance and reach here soon." Virushali replied and showed her phone. "I really feel bad for Nila, not sure why god is testing her this much." Anitha said eyeing the unconscious Nila.

In few hours Aradhana returned and checked Nila. "Doctor says it will take more than 3 hours to say the condition him. What got into her, never she hurt someone like this before?" Aradhana said closing her eyes tight. "Once Nila wakes let's take her to him. She has all the rights to know the truth, enough of the pain and worries she went through" Virushali said. Anitha enquired about the work Aradhana and Jannvi went. "They looked like a big network, we killed 6 of them and arrested the rest. Took over all the evidence from their side. We never expected such a gang behind us Anitha ma. But if we haven't received the information on time, we would have lost everything including Nila." Jannvi said.

Nila woke up, her head pained like hell. She tried to stand up but she fell down. Hearing the sound all 4 rushed to the room. Finding Nila lying on the floor, Aradhana nearly shouted "Nila", carrying her in her arms she made Nila to lie on the bed. "Nila ma, open your eyes. We are all here. See us Nila. We are here near you. All your prayers are answered, we are safe and sound", Aradhana spoke with tears in her eyes. Jannvi tapped Aradhana's shoulder comforting her. Anitha bought a bowl of warm water, Virushali soaked a fluffy towel in the warm water and cleaned her face and hands. Slowly Nila opened her eyes. Her face slowly turned from calm and anger. Aradhana resisted Nila from getting up. "Take rest Nila ma" said Aradhana. "I have to kill that bastard Aradhana, I can't rest until I take his life" Nila spoke catching her irregular breaths. "Who do you think he is?", Anitha asked angrily. "He is..." Nila stammered to answer. "He is your Mugilan Nila. Your Mugilan..." Aradhana spoke taking Nila's hand into her's. "Mugilan" Nila's lips spelled his name and her eyes slowly shut down taking her into the deep sleep.

11

"Fear Not Baby Girl"

Nila was admitted to hospital, she fell into coma. Her mind couldn't take up too much and it locked itself from the reality. Mugilan got saved from the brim of death. May be Nila was praying for him even in her coma state. Mugilan got discharged in 2 days. His right hand fingers and left shoulder was slowly healing with the medicines and physio. His head injury was still in diagnosis. After complete rest of four days, Mugilan was allowed to visit Nila.

Entering in Mugilan found his Nila lying in the bed with some monitors connected to her. Sitting next to her, holding her hands all he was able to do is shed those tears. It's all his mistake. He should have revealed the truth the moment he came to Chennai day before their birthday, but he had his reasons to stay under the cover. Kissing her knuckles, he came out. Aradhana who was waiting out just gave a tap on his shoulders.

Next day, after getting some flowers in the flower shop Mugilan visited the hospital. Entering in he pulled himself together. Keeping the flowers near her head, he spoke, "I miss you Nila ma, I always wished to be with you. Things were going good until I found that Aravindan was following me. After meeting him everything changed upside down. I am sorry Nila ma. I made you go through this much." He cried his heart out holding her hands. Slowly caressing her hair, he placed a long kiss on her forehead. He left unable to see her in an unresponsive condition. But here Nila started to gain her conscious. All her mind waited was for the call of her Mugilan. Once hearing it, it woke up. Doctor called Nila's father finding her gaining conscious. Mugilan haven't turned up even after hearing the news. Even Mugilan's parents haven't got any idea why he is not visiting Nila.

After a day, four girls came to see Nila. "How are you feeling Nila", as Aradhana asked Nila nodded her head. "Anitha help me with my hair, it's very clumsy da" as Nila asked Anitha started doing her hair. "I think now you guys can tell me what actually happened. And where is Mugilan, I am waiting for him actually." Nila asked. Virushali answered, "Actually we are also waiting for Mugilan to visit you. We have only one side of story. We don't know things that happened in Mugilan's home town." Nila signed and took the water bottle from her side table. "Who saved you on that night, I really thought I lost you guys and why you people haven't contacted me back once rescued?" Nila asked after gulping some water. Aradhana started their side of story.

That night when they were attacked, there came a masked man who rescued the four girls. They were moved to a safe place, and only after that they got to know that the one who rescued them is the friend of Mugilan. Girls understood that Mugilan is planning something behind

Nila. Mugilan's friend asked the girls to wait until they receive a location message from Mugilan. After 2 days, they received a message from Mugilan with the location of their safe house. Mugilan's friend advised them about the live nano camera in his eyes and voice transmitter in his ear. But unfortunately before they reach, Nila took the half-life Mugilan. Hearing all these, Nila remembered how he was texting something without watching the phone screen. She scolded herself for beating the life out of him. She felt bad for not respecting the raised doubt from the start. Some tears made way to the hospital sheets covering her.

Doctor asked her to be on observation until next day morning. Once the visitors time got over, everyone left. Thinking about why Mugilan was not visiting her, Nila dozed off even before 6.00 PM.

Feeling something insecure, she woke up trying to get the gun under her pillow. Once the reality slapped, she realized that she is in hospital and she doesn't have a gun now. Checking the room, she found nothing unusual. After lying down she felt someone caressing her hair. Turing around she found Mugilan standing there. The half-moon's light was no giving much vision but Nila was very sure that was Mugilan. He helped Nila to get up. He checked her hurts and found everything was healed. "How about a long drive Nila?" as soon as he asked, Nila hugged him. "No drive needed Mugilan, I just needed your nearness", Nila pressed her face into his chest.

Mugilan sat next to her taking her in his lap. Nila stayed silent for few minutes. Mugilan slowly played with her hair. Nila broke the silence, "What happened in your home town Mugilan?". He took a deep breath. Staring at the wall, he began to narrate his side of "story".

When Mugilan reached his hometown he first started to spend some time with his parents and friends. But every time he came out, he felt like being watched. With the help of his friends he found that a masked man is following and found that man's staying place. Mugilan decided to surprise that masked man and paid a visit. But he was taken by surprise seeing the man being exact copy of himself. After a few bullet firing, punches and bleeding nose Aravindan confessed the truth. It looked like he planned to change his medicines and sedate him, and replace his position. Later with the help of his gang he will take down the Nila team and handover the project details to those selfish bastards. After getting the truths from him, Mugilan with the help of his friends tied Aravindan in the same house and started to communicate with the opposite gang like Aravindan replaced Mugilan. They decided to keep Aravindan under cover until they bring every one behind this out. But unfortunately within 2 days while Aravindan tried to escape Mugilan himself shot him taking his life away. On the day Mugilan started from his hometown, the opposite gang called him and fixed him with the voice transmitter and nano camera. It resisted him from telling the plan to Nila. He acted well keeping the gang busy, unexpected thing is that Nila falling into the hands of anxiety.

Once Mugilan explained things, Nila slowly woke up from his lap. "Sorry Mugil, for dragging you into this." Mugilan placed his silence finger on her lips and told, "No more discussion on past Nila ma, all I need is the present and future filled with our Love." She sweetly nodded earning a kiss from Mugilan.

Mugilan and Nila both got moved from the incidents little faster because of the immediate marriage date declared by Mugilan's mother. Purchasing and arrangements kept them busy from discussing their professional things. Mugilan was asked to join in work just one week after the marriage, so Mugilan was planning a good one week stay which Nila could never forget in her life. Nila was already assigned to an assignment, her team started to gather the details they needed and waited for Nila to join them. 8

Just two days in mid for the marriage, Mugilan wished to talk with Nila. Informing Nila's father, he took Nila for a drive. Night stars were adoring the beautiful couple. The night breeze embraced them, making Nila to hug the Mugilan who was driving. Mugilan was smiling thanking the stars and moon which blessed them to be a couple. Reaching the beach, Nila said, "You planned to bring me to beach in this cold wind, very bad idea Mugi ma". Mugilan smiled at her statement, "Nila ma, see those waves are scolding you badly and moving away from you". Nila gave a stern look at him and asked, "Why will they scold me". "They are scolding you as an unromantic fellow Nila ma, I bought you even in this breeze because You have me to warm you as much as you needed" Mugilan said hugging her from behind. His warmth and nearness made her cheeks red.

Nila took his hand into hers and pressed a kiss on his knuckles. They stayed silent observing the Moon. Nila spoke eyeing the waves which was sharing secrets of ocean to the sand, "Spit out the words Mugi ma, I know you have bought me here to tell something important".

"Nila ma, you are happy right", Mugilan asked making her comfortably sit on the sand. "What sort of question is this Mugi, I am happy can't you see that?" Nila replied hooking her right hand with his left hand. "I could see that you are happy Nila ma, but there is also a hint of fear in those eyes whenever you are alone and away from me. Tell me Nila what's bothering you?". Nila stayed silent and averted her face away from Mugilan. Waiting for few minutes, Mugilan himself turned her face towards him. He was not surprised by her tears, wiping her tears away he slowly side hugged her.

"Unless you let me in, I will not able to see what you are going through Nila ma. It's just me, you and it's all about being us. What is the reason for your fear, Please Nila ma don't cry," Mugilan said again wiping those unstoppable tears of her. "I am afraid of our professions Mugi, luckily last time you survived Aravindan's plan what if something happened wrong to you. Not every time our instincts help us Mugi. What if I myself killed you on that day in the basement? How the hell would I be moving from the moments I hurt you with my own hands. Still some pieces of my conscious is warning you as Aravindan, Still I am struck in that basement with that heightened rush to take your life away from you. I am going mad with these fear ruling in my mind." Nila said observing the facial changes of Mugilan as she was confessing.

"Fear not my baby girl. What if the instincts don't help us, our love will always save us Nila ma. You always say right? you have your prayers for me. That will help me from any danger I face. My prayers will save you. Just think Nila ma, our love is not like other simple ones. I have been accompanying you from the moment you born. You are born for me as I am born for you. I have been waiting to share my life time with you since the moment my father revealed about us. Don't consider the things that happened on the last mission. You would have never killed me, because deep under your heart you know that's me. Your detective mind triggered your rage and your mind believed the words that Mugilan was no more. That's actually the best evidence of how much you loved me and how much long leaps you will make for me. I feel lucky Nila ma, for taking the pleasure to witness the love you had for me. Fear not Nila ma, leave the past. Promise me to share your present and future with me." Mugilan spoke and Nila hugged him tight as he asked the promise. "I promise you Mugi, I will always be there with you." Nila said. The White moon and Black clouds witnessing the beautiful love story embraced each other just as Mugilan and Nila.

Dropping Nila at home, Mugilan returned back to his room. He heard his phone ringing in the cupboard of the room. He attended the call and spoke, "Yes, Aravindan here."